Until We Meet Again

Story by Susan Jones

Illustrations by Shirley Antak

50/50 PUBLISHING

MINNEAPOLIS, MINNESOTA

UNTIL WE MEET AGAIN
Copyright 2007 by Susan Jones

Illustrated by Shirley Antak

This book is a work of fiction.
Names, characters, places and incidents
are products of the author's imagination.
Any resemblance to actual events or persons,
living or dead, is entirely coincidental.

50)50 PUBLISHING

50|50 Publishing
Soulo Communications
2617 East Hennepin Avenue
Minneapolis, MN 55413

To order, visit www.50-50publishing.com
Reseller discounts available.

Printed in Canada

First Edition: February 2007
11 10 09 08 07   1 2 3 4 5
Design and typesetting by Thomas Heller, Mori Studio Inc.

ISBN 13: 978-0-9778209-4-8
ISBN 10: 0-9778209-4-7

Library of Congress Control Number:
2007922455

To my father, Earl Jones,
who I know found peace during his
final journey home and whose whisper,
"Until we meet again"
continues to bring
me comfort.

My grandfather lived in the house next door. He had been there as long as I could remember and he was my best friend in the whole world.

Whenever I walked in the door, Grandpa always met me with a big smile, looked me in the eye and tapped me on the tip of my nose.

(Grandpa said, "That's to let you know how special you are.")

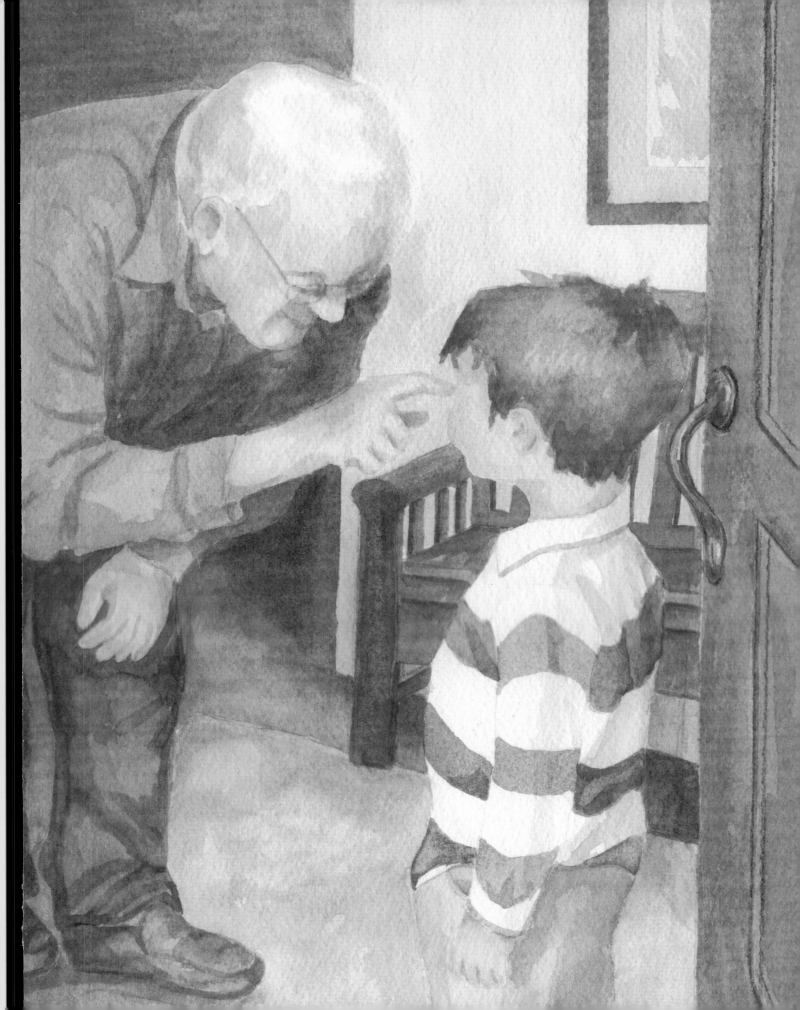

We did lots of fun things like playing games together. Sometimes I won and sometimes he won. We never stopped until the game had a winner.

(Grandpa said, "Never cheat, but play fair and always finish the game.")

Grandpa told stories. I loved to hear about when he was a little boy. He had five brothers and they really knew how to share everything.

(Grandpa said, "Never take the biggest piece of anything. Take the smallest one and tomorrow there will be something left to share.")

Grandpa played the piano. As he played, we sang silly old songs together. Sometimes I would dance and jump around.

(Grandpa said, "You can't be sad if you're acting silly.")

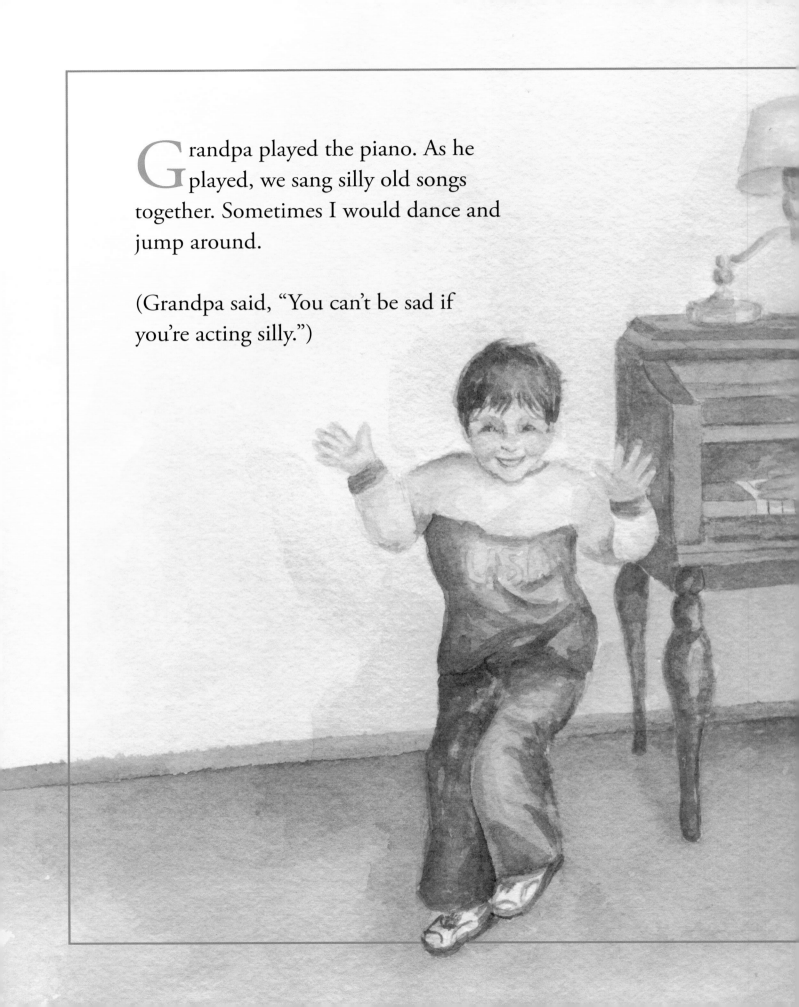

Grandpa taught me things too, like learning how to wink. It wasn't easy and Grandpa had to show me many times.

First, I just blinked with both eyes. Now I can wink one or the other.

(Grandpa said, "A wink means we are in this together.")

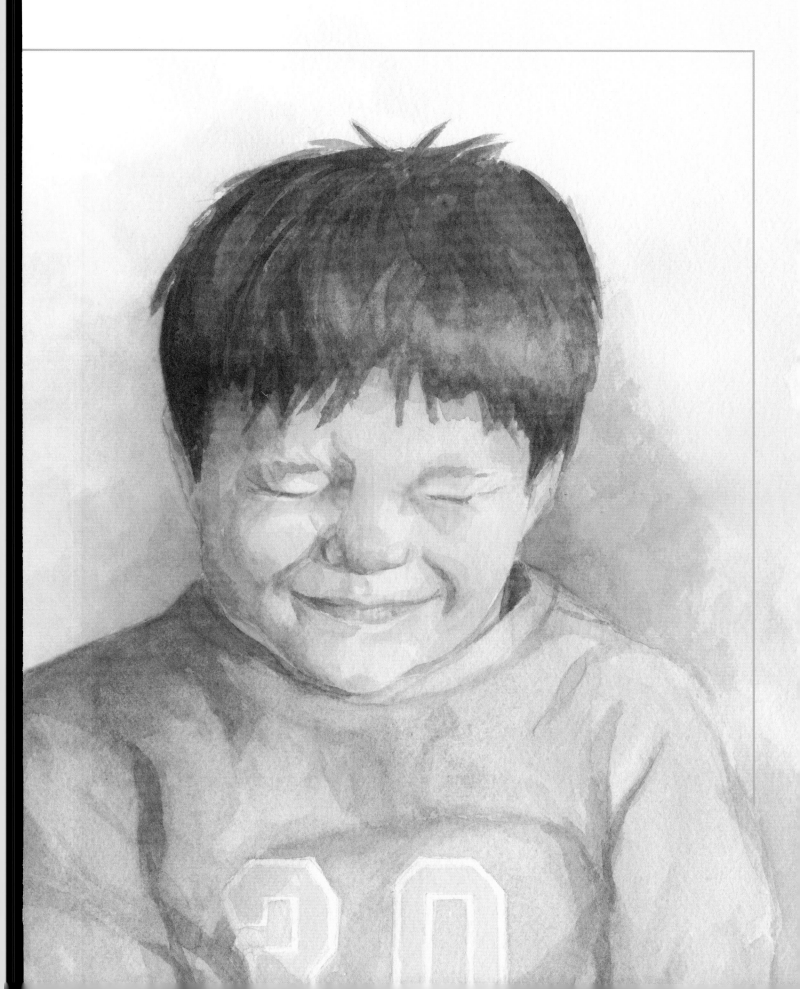

Grandpa liked hot chocolate. He showed me how to float marshmallows on top and make a chocolate moustache.

(Grandpa said, "Hot chocolate warms the heart like nothing else can.")

Grandpa gave big hugs—strong ones that lifted me right up off the ground.

(Grandpa said, "Hugs are magical because you get one back whenever you give one away.")

Grandpa loved balloons—bright, fat balloons. We would blow them up until we were out of breath. Then we would take them to the park and give them all away.

On breezy days the wind carried many balloons. Some drifted left and fell to the ground. Some drifted right and fell to the ground. But a few rode the wind—floating up, up, up into the sky until they were too small to see.

(Grandpa said, "Every time a balloon gets away it's like someone's floating up to Heaven.")

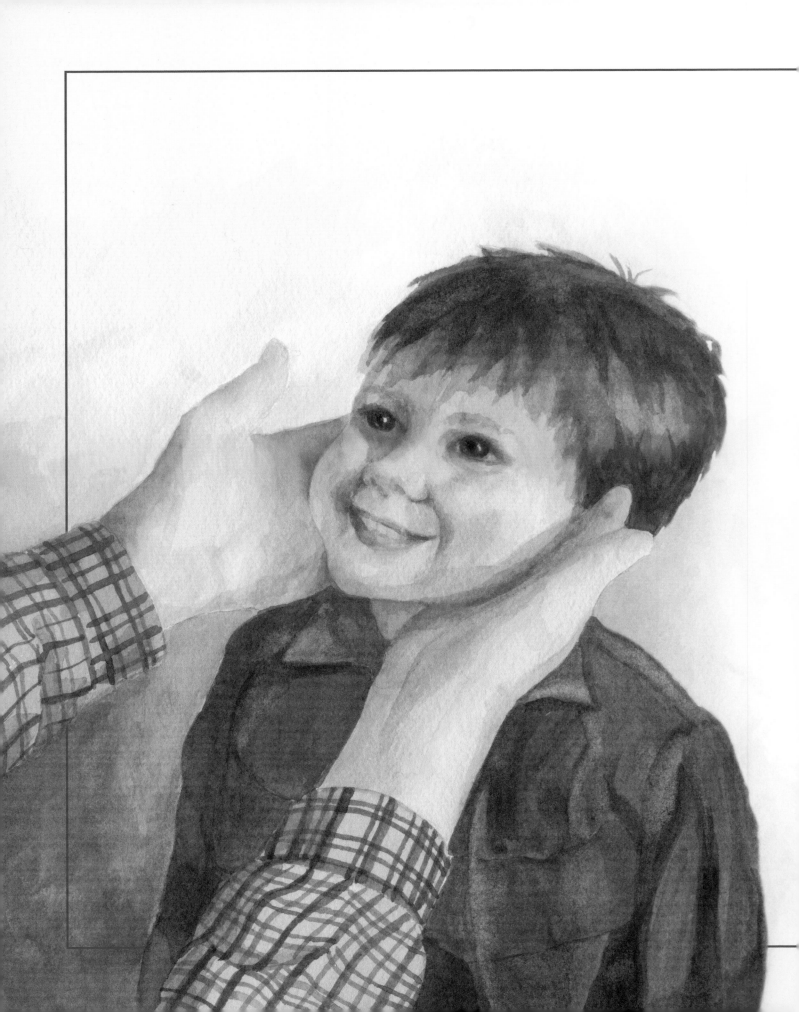

When it was time for me to go home, Grandpa would always hold my face in his hands, kiss my forehead and say in his strong voice, "Until we meet again."

I would look up and, in *my* strongest voice, say back to him, "Until we meet again."

Then, one day when I went to Grandpa's house after school, he didn't meet me at the door with his big smile. Instead, I was surprised my mama opened the door.

I stepped inside and saw my grandpa sitting in his big, old chair where we played games. He looked tired and a little sad.

Hoping to cheer him up, I asked him to play the piano, but Grandpa said he wasn't feeling well. He told me he was very sick.

So I hugged him with a magical hug and said my smiles would make him better. Grandpa hugged me back and said he wished that could be true, but soon he would be too sick to play games or sing silly songs.

I asked him what would happen then. He said someday—but not today—he would get too weak to even breathe.

I looked at my mama to help me understand. She told me, when that day came, Grandpa would go away to a beautiful place called Heaven. And once he got to Heaven, he wouldn't be sick anymore. Or tired. Or sad.

But I told my grandpa he couldn't go away. Not without me. I told him we would go together.

Grandpa shook his head and smiled a tired smile. He said I couldn't go because I still had many games to play and silly songs to sing.

Then my grandpa asked me a question. He asked me to tell him what we had done together the day before. I told him we made popcorn and played a game of checkers.

"That," said Grandpa, "is called a memory. You and I have lots of them—one for everything we have ever done together. They are all around you. They are in your heart. And that is where I will be. That is where you will find me... until we meet again."

Mama brought us some hot chocolate and I sat down beside my grandpa's chair. I thought about all the things we had done together. I thought how every night, when I went home for supper, Grandpa said, "Until we meet again."

"But until then," I said, looking up at Grandpa, "we have more memories to make."

I tapped him on the tip of his nose to let him know how special he was and said, "Let's make a list of *new* memories to make your heart smile—no matter how tired you get."

And we did.

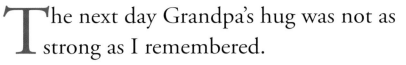

The next day Grandpa's hug was not as strong as I remembered.

The day after that he was too tired to tell stories or sing silly songs.

And then, one day, Grandpa fell asleep in his chair while we were playing a game.

Mama came over and gave me a hug. She said, "Maybe it's time to look at that list you and Grandpa made together."

I reached into my pocket and felt the folded paper. While Grandpa slept, I counted all the new memories we had decided could make his heart smile. There were so many!

When it started to get dark, I found Grandpa's favorite blanket and tucked it around him in his chair. Then I kissed him on the forehead and whispered, "Until we meet again."

Every day after that, I made a new and perfect memory for my grandpa. Sometimes I would dance and make him laugh as I jumped around.

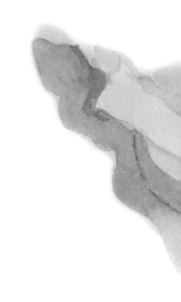

play games
sing
Be silly
drink
hot chocalat
wink
laugh
hugs
popcorn
have fun

Other times, I would hug him as best I could and his head would rest on my shoulder.

Sometimes I wasn't sure my grandpa was awake, but then he would smile when I whispered, "I love you."

I sang our silly old songs. I told him stories about a little boy who learned the best things ever from his grandpa. (Like never cheat. Always share. And hugs are magical.)

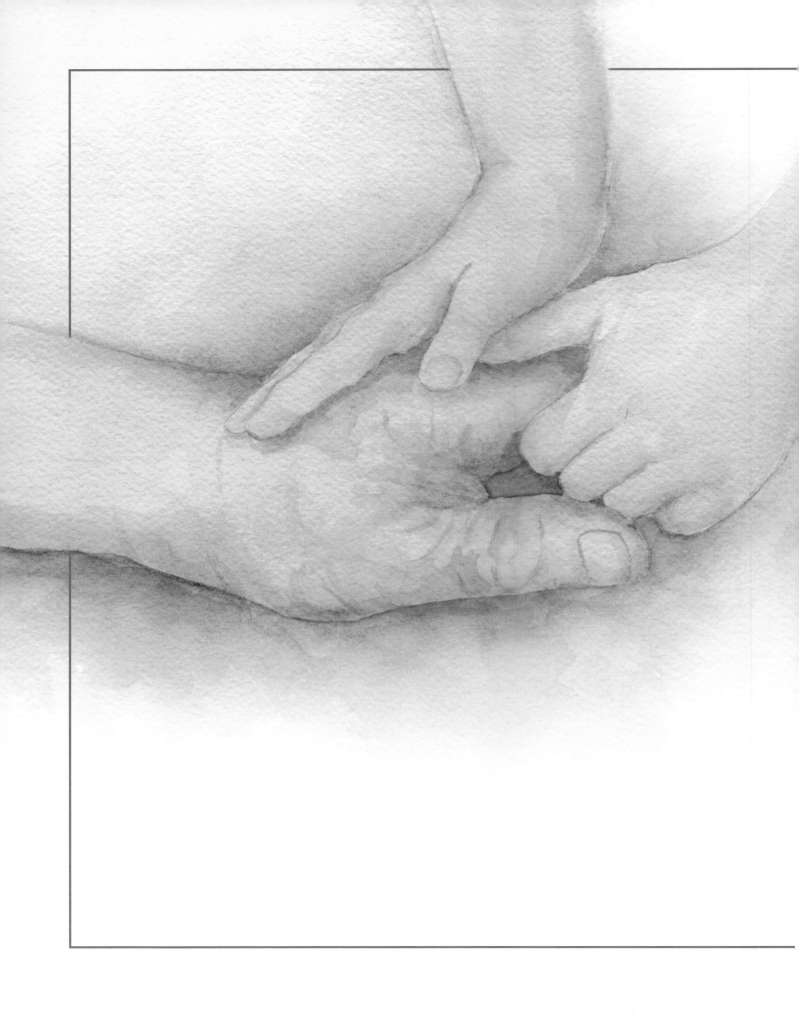

I held his hands when they got shaky. And I made sure my touch was ever so gentle. I hummed to him when he was too tired to talk.

I tapped the tip of his nose—just like he used to touch mine—so he would know how special he was to me.

Sometimes I would give him a wink—even when his eyes were closed—to remind him we were in this together.

And each day, when it was time for me to go home, I would hold Grandpa's face in my hands, just like he used to hold mine. I would kiss his forehead and say, in my bravest voice, "Until we meet again."

And he would whisper back to me, "Until we meet again…"

One day, I gave my grandpa a balloon. After he tried to hold it, I tied it to his bed. I told him I could imagine him floating up to Heaven, just like a balloon floats up into the sky.

And I told him I would be okay, because everything we ever did together was in my heart. I even promised I would tap myself on the tip of my nose for him and listen to the memories we made together.

It wasn't that day or the next, but it wasn't long until Grandpa floated up to Heaven like a balloon. I cried and cried. My grandpa was gone.

There were no more things on the list I could do to make his heart smile and I missed him so much.

His big, old chair was empty. And his piano didn't make a sound.

That's when I remembered my promise.

So I tapped myself on the tip of my nose and I listened.

I listened hard in the quiet room where we had laughed and played games and sang silly songs.

And I heard my grandpa's whisper
ever-so-softly in my heart,
"Until we meet again, child.
Until we meet again."

That was many, many years ago—so long ago that I am a grandpa now, with a grandson of my own.

Some nights I get to tuck him into bed after the silly songs and the games. I tap him gently on the nose, look into his sleepy eyes and say, "Until we meet again." And right there in the quiet dark I hear a whisper in my heart. It is my own grandpa's smiling voice. "Until we meet again, child. Until we meet again."

Gratitudes

I am grateful to many for bringing this tender story to life. Without you it would still be simple jottings from an early-morning, waking dream. Special thanks to

- My editor Suzanne Foust, for your kindred spirit and faithfulness to my story.

- Friend and illustrator Shirley Antak, whose gifts and collaboration made a little boy and his grandfather come alive before my eyes.

- Photographer Erin Antak and models Dick Jones and Gavin McCabe, for your willing, wonderful work behind the scenes.

- My parents, Loraine and Earl Jones for all the treasured memories.

- My precious sister Molly, for comforting our father and giving him a daughter's farewell.

- My brother Roger, for your gift of laughter, making ordinary moments memorable.

- My Uncle Clayton and dear friend Rick Moore, for your loving support and unwavering belief in me.

- Devoted friend, Carol Knott for being a treasured part of this journey.

- Compassionate caregivers who graced our lives with kindness and wisdom.

- And to you who are holding this book… may the love between a little boy and his grandfather open your heart to memory-making that celebrates relationships and helps us live with loss.